Old Friends
(ENDLESS LOVE)

William McDonald

Copyright © 2016 by William McDonald
All rights reserved. No part of this book may be reproduced, scanned, or distributed in any printed or electronic form without permission.
First Edition: February 2016
Printed in the United States of America
ISBN: 9781682733066
ISBN: 1682733068

**OLD FRIENDS
(ENDLESS LOVE)**

© 2016 by William McDonald

Cover Photo: iStock

Cover Design: Scott Woldin

This book is a work of fiction. Names, characters, locations and incidents are products of the author's imagination. Any resemblance to actual persons, living or dead is entirely coincidental.

Praise For Old Friends (Endless Love)

"I love how the (writing) gives the stories a rhythm like a song. The words are beautiful and the messages powerful." JoLee W/Boulder

"Evocative and touching. Rich and full of imagery with a hopefulness that really touched my heart." Kris M/Kauai

"Absolutely amazing and magical and beautiful! I'm bawling my head off and am covered in goosebumps!!!" Betsy C/Idaho

"A beautiful, touching book." Raymond H/Alaska

"These warm and tender portrayals of enduring love are uplifting and reassuring. They brought a tear to my eye and a smile to my heart." Patricia S/Oro Valley

"I spent the first week of this year in the hospital and read your stories over and over. They are beautiful, heart wrenching and unforgettable. They helped get me through a tough time in my life." Mary B/Winnipeg, Canada

"A lovely book, written with true illuminating grace." Christine/Chicago

There are too many millions of elderly women and men looking for an escape from the loss and loneliness of growing old alone.

This book is for every one of you.

When I am old.

When I begin to curl at the edges like something left too long in the sun.

When I am holding to life like a lamp holding to the last drop of oil.

When I will pass most of my time alone, I hope to be in the company of men and women such as those who inspired these unique love stories; old friends who taught me every day the true meaning of courage, dignity, honor, grace and faith.

Who still believe and make me believe that anything is possible at any age.

Even love.

William McDonald

I believe the need for love is the most powerful and driving motivation known to man.

And woman.

It can break your heart, and it can break your heart wide open. Either way, when we're living without it, it feels like we're living only half a life.

Maybe that's what makes these stories so unique?

They touch our humanity and speak to our hearts and souls of what we seek from the first moment we draw breath.

Love.

And as much as we may have, we always want more.

Mari Devon

This book would not be complete without the thoughts, suggestions and poetic wordplay of Mari Devon. Thank you, Mari.

I believe in getting your eyes fixed if you have cataracts because it doesn't matter how old you get there's still plenty to see.

       Doc, who is 84 and sees a lot more than
           anyone thinks he does.

Franklin and Rebecca

Franklin lived in 210.

Rebecca lived in 211.

It wasn't always that way. But that's another story.

They met in the hall one morning on their way to breakfast.

Franklin, on the arm of his caregiver, bowed his head slightly, smiled and said, "Good morning. Do you know you have beautiful eyes?"

Rebecca, on the arm of her caregiver, smiled back and said, "Good morning. Do you know you have a lovely smile?"

Franklin smiled again.

Nothing more was said until they reached the elevator, where Rebecca whispered to her caregiver, "What's his name? He has a lovely smile."

"His name is Franklin," the caregiver whispered back.

"Who is she?" Franklin whispered to his caregiver. "She has beautiful eyes."

"Her name is Rebecca," the caregiver whispered back.

After breakfast, Franklin, on the arm of his caregiver, returned to 210. Rebecca, on the arm of her caregiver, returned to 211.

Franklin spent the rest of the morning very patiently unfolding the piece of paper he kept in a small wooden box by the window, reading it, then very precisely refolding it and returning it to the small wooden box.

There were nine delicately handwritten words on the piece of paper.

> *When I can no longer remember you … remember me.*

Always the same thought ran through Franklin's mind - remember who? Sometimes, like a faraway light in a deep, dark place, a thought valiantly fought its way toward him but just when it was within reach and he tried to grasp it, it burst like a bubble.

A man named Samuel had given him the box with the note in it, but Franklin did not remember that. Nor did he remember that Samuel was his son.

Across the hall, in 211, Rebecca sat in her favorite chair — a La-Z-Boy Veranda stationary chair. Rebecca didn't know that. Nor did she know that Elizabeth, the woman who gave her the chair, was her daughter.

But Rebecca did love to sit in that La-Z-Boy Veranda stationary chair, as quiet as a dove on her nest, and stare out the window.

They met again in the hall on their way to dinner.

Franklin, on the arm of his caregiver, bowed his head slightly, smiled and said, "Good morning. Do you know you have beautiful eyes?"

Rebecca, on the arm of her caregiver, smiled back and said, "Good morning. Do you know you have a lovely smile?"

Old Friends

Franklin smiled again.

Neither caregiver chose to remind them that it was evening.

Getting onto the elevator, their hands accidentally touched.

Rebecca felt something – didn't know what, but in the darkness, something seemed to be reaching out.

Franklin felt something – didn't know what, but in his confusion, an answer seemed to be trying to make its way toward him, but just when it was within reach and he tried to grasp it, it burst like a bubble.

Nothing more was said until the elevator doors closed and Rebecca whispered to her caregiver, "What's his name? He has a lovely smile."

"His name is Franklin," the caregiver whispered back.

And Franklin whispered to his caregiver, "Who is she? She has beautiful eyes."

"Her name is Rebecca," the caregiver whispered back.

After dinner, Franklin, on the arm of his caregiver, returned to 210 where he spent the rest of the evening very patiently unfolding the piece of paper he kept in a small wooden box by the window, reading it, then very precisely refolding it and returning it to the small wooden box.

> *When I can no longer remember you ... remember me.*

Rebecca, on the arm of her caregiver, returned to 211 and spent the rest of the evening in her favorite chair, the La-Z-Boy Veranda stationary chair, sitting, as quiet as a dove on her nest, staring out the window.

And so it went, day after day.

Franklin's son, Samuel, visited his father often.

Rebecca's daughter, Elizabeth, visited her mother just as often.

Sometimes they ate together, and always, Franklin would ask, "Who is she? She has beautiful eyes."

"Her name is Rebecca, Dad, and you're right, she does have beautiful eyes."

And always, Rebecca would ask her daughter, "Who is he? He has a lovely smile."

"His name is Franklin, Mother, and yes, he does have a lovely smile."

Franklin was the first to go, passing quietly one December morning. Only a day later, Rebecca, in her favorite chair, closed her eyes and, like Franklin, gently stepped from this life to the next.

The notice in the newspaper said that Franklin and Rebecca had been married nearly 60 years, had two children, Elizabeth and Samuel, and more grandchildren and great-grandchildren than they knew of.

Epilogue

On a December morning, Rebecca found herself walking through a field of wildflowers, unlike any she'd ever seen. Someone had told her they were called Godsend. In the middle of the field, she saw Franklin, waiting to welcome her.

"Remember me, Franklin?" Rebecca asked.

"Always, Rebecca." Franklin answered. "Do you know you have beautiful eyes?"

"Do you know you have a lovely smile?"

Looking around, she asked, "Is this heaven?"

Franklin smiled and answered, "It is now."

You can't plan your life. It just happens.
              Barbara, who is 94 and greets every day
                            like a long-lost friend.

Anna's Tree

It was cold.
    Canada cold.
Minnesota cold.
Dakota cold.
Everything.
Everywhere.
In a deep freeze.

There was a wind.
Howling.
Prowling.
Razor sharp.
Like the teeth of the walleye slumbering near the bottom of the ice-covered bay. The coyotes howled, but only halfheartedly, and somewhere there was a bear saying, "Wake me when it's over."

Not a night to be outside.
He was.

He limped.
The cane helped, but not much.
He could hear her voice in the wind. "You think you're made of concrete, old man? You're made of dust. Stay home."
"But I must go, Anna. I must tend to the tree."

She would cluck a little longer, a little louder.
Then kiss him and make tea and wait by the window for his return.
He smiled.
How he loved that woman.

The "tree" was a Lavender Twist Weeping Redbud. Anna had pointed it out to him in one of the magazines at the doctor's office.

"Look, old man, this is a tree! Look how it flowers, look how it bows so low to the earth, spreading its arms like an umbrella, protecting everything within its shadow. THIS, this is a tree unlike any tree to be found between all the oceans!"

And so he had bought one.

He called it Anna's tree.
And on this winter night it needed tending.
He'd heard that weather like this could split the trunk like it was a matchstick. That would end everything. He would start over if he had to, plant a new tree if he had to, but in his heart he knew this was the one for the job.

"At least it's not snowing," he muttered, trying to warm himself with the thought.
It started to snow.
He shivered and struggled on, the wind going through him like he wasn't even there, snapping at his bad leg like a rabid dog.

It took him awhile. Things looked different in the night, in the snow, in the half-moon, but he found it, fell to his knees and wrapped his hands around the young trunk of Anna's tree. Feeling how strong and defiant it was, he could only smile and whisper, "You see, Anna? This is a good one. This is the one for the job."

Old Friends

Still, not willing to take any chance that winter would get the best of things the minute he turned his back, the old man removed the worn woolen scarf from around his neck and wrapped it tightly around the trunk of the brave young tree.

Then he rose and made his way home.
Through the wind.
And the snow.
And the cold.
And the half-moon.
Pausing at the doorstep, he could hear her.

"You tied your scarf around a tree?"
And she would cluck like a hen for at least an hour.
But in between, she would kiss him and serve tea.
He smiled, breathed deeply, sighed even more deeply and went inside.
How he loved that woman.

The walk had tired him more than he thought it would. He could hear Anna.

"What man alive does not think he can do all that he did in his youth? Even a bent-down old man with eyes that water, a nose that runs and legs that fight to hold him up. I'll make tea."

He slept.
Dreamed of other days.
Warmer, softer days.
Of rivers lighted by the moon, of fireflies, nightingales and loons on the bay.

And while he slept and dreamed, the rains came.
Winter rains, clinging to everything they touched until everything they touched turned to ice.

He woke.
Looked out at the frozen world and knew he had to return to the tree. Ice like this could break the backs of those young branches, snap them like they were twigs in a campfire.

Stepping outside, he could hear her.
"You'll slip and fall, old man, and they'll find your bones in a coyote's belly!"
"But I must tend to the tree, Anna."
She would cluck a little more.
Then kiss him and make tea and wait by the window for his return.
He smiled.
How he loved that woman.

It took him longer to get to Anna's tree than it had the night before.
He fell twice, landing once on his bad leg, once on his good leg.

By the time he got to it, the tree was bent dangerously, awkwardly close to the ground, no match for the weight of the frozen winter rain. The old man flailed at the tree with his cane for nearly an hour until finally, other than one branch that would have to fight for its life, the ice was gone and Anna's tree seemed to breathe a sigh of relief. He took his cane and propped it under the weakened branch.

"You have a job to do. Don't give up."

Exhausted, he limped home.
The winds blew.
The snow deepened.
The ice thickened.
Winter stayed longer than usual.
The coyotes howled in protest.

The tree, Anna's tree, never gave up.
Finally, it was spring.

Old Friends

The world changed color.
Blue grass.
African violet.
Irish moss.
Black-eyed Susan.
Marigold.

Anna's tree was doing everything a Lavender Twist Weeping Redbud should do. The weeping, twisted branches tipped toward the ground and spread out like an umbrella, protecting everything within its shadow. The lavender pink flowers and reddish-purple heart-shaped leaves shone in the sun and danced in the breeze.

The old man was pleased. "You were, right, Anna. Unlike any tree to be found between all the oceans."

He stepped back to admire the tree, a worn woolen scarf still tied around its trunk, a cane still propping up one of the branches, but doing the job it had been planted to do – watch over a simple gravestone with just one word on it.

ANNA

He smiled, turned and limped away.
He'd be back tomorrow.
To tend to the tree.
Anna's tree.
How he loved that woman.

Faith

*I*s **May-Beth**, who has a broken back that will never heal and a spirit that will never break. May-Beth, who sings *Jesus Loves Me* — loudly, without a thought to who's listening. Or who isn't.

Edna's Hands

She has a gentleness that almost seems holy, a voice that could calm a storm. A peace, like the kind you'd find in a country church on a Saturday morning, follows her everywhere. On a cold day you could warm yourself just by sitting next to her.

Her name is Marti and she is on loan from heaven.

She cares for people who are older.
Frail.
People who feel helpless.
Useless.
Used up.
Unimportant.
And she makes them realize how much more they have to offer to anyone with sense enough to listen.

This morning Marti, peace and grace, is with Edna, fire and smoke.

"How are you feeling this morning, Edna?" Marti asks in a voice that could calm a storm.
"Old." Edna answers, in a voice that sounds like a storm brewing. "I'm feeling old. I'm a bent-down old woman with runny eyes."
"You're not old, Edna. You're aging."
"Honey, I'm not aging, I'm drying up."
"How are your hands?"

William McDonald

"They're old too."
"Are they hurting today?"
"They hurt every day."

Marti takes Edna's hands in her own and begins to massage them. Edna falls silent. For several minutes, she watches as Marti slowly, gently massages some of the pain away. Finally, in a soft, sad voice, she says, "Look at my hands. Old, hurting, wrinkled, gnarled and useless."

"That's not what I see," Marti answers. Not stopping the massage, not taking her eyes off Edna's hands, she continues. "I look at your hands and I wonder how many tears have they wiped from the face of a child? How many bandages have they put on scraped knees? How many times have they cradled the face of the man you loved? Caressed the faces of the children you have loved? How many gardens have they planted? How many spring bouquets have they gathered? I look at your hands and I wonder how many meals have they prepared?"

She looks up. Edna has drifted to a faraway place.

Remembering.
Re-loving.
Reliving a thousand moments in time.

"I look at your hands, Edna, and I wonder how many times have they counted nickels and pennies hoping they would add up to enough to get through another month? How many times have you run those hands through your hair wondering if you're doing everything right? Or wrong? How many baby blankets have they knit for how many grandchildren? How many times have they been folded in prayer? I look at your hands, Edna, and I see a lifetime."
Marti, peace and grace, looks up.
Edna, fire and smoke. has tears in her eyes.

Old Friends

"Yeah, yeah, I know, I'm blubbering," Edna says.

"I don't see tears in your eyes, Edna," Marti answers in a voice that could calm a storm. "Let me tell you what I see in your eyes."

And she smiles.
And Edna smiles.

And waits for the words that will make her realize how very alive she still is.

Words from a woman with a voice that could calm a storm.

I could be married again. I don't want to be, but I could be, because I've still got it.
        Ted, who is 85 and likes to sit at the ladies' table.

Too Old to Love

I am still in love with the love of my life.

It is a love as fresh as its first day.

All those years ago.

The experts tell me I am too old to experience those same joys of love, that the emotions I felt then are now just symptoms of one medical disorder or another.

When a mere glance from the love of my life sets my heart racing, the experts tell me it is just a side effect of the Levaquin I've been taking for my sinus infections or that my Tenormin dosage may need adjusting.

When I look into the eyes of the love of my life - eyes that have seen me at my best and at my worst and never looked away, eyes that have told me a thousand times how much I am loved, I am still, after all these years, at a complete loss for words. The experts tell me that it may be an early sign of Alzheimer's and that they'd like to put me on a light regimen of Razadyne.

When just one gentle touch from the love of my life makes me go weak at the knees, the experts tell me that it is a symptom of a too sedentary lifestyle and that I should consider a yoga class for seniors, preferably one that offers the half moon pose.

William McDonald

When I hear the breeze in the trees whisper the name of the love of my life, the experts tell me that audio delirium is sometimes associated with poor hearing and that I should look into getting hearing aids.

When I look at the love of my life and, after all these years, I still see only the person I have made perfect in my eyes throughout a lifetime, the person to whom I promised the moon and the stars but loved me as though she had just inherited the earth, the experts tell me that while the Ambien I take can offer much-needed relief for people with sleep disorders, they caution that newly reported side effects may explain my lack of accepting reality.

When the love of my life smiles the smile that has lit the way through so many dark days, it still leaves me breathless. The experts tell me that I may have developed an airway obstruction, common with most people my age.

When just thinking about the love of my life makes me warm all over and has me walking around with a silly grin on my face, the experts tell me that it's possible I am in a heat-induced daze, impairing my judgment; perhaps I should have the air conditioner checked or walk around inside an air-conditioned mall for an hour or so?

When I insist that I am as madly in love with this woman as I was all those years ago, the experts tell me experiments on lovebirds found that their serotonin levels were equivalent to the low serotonin levels found in sufferers of obsessive-compulsive disorder.

When the love of my life hugs me the way I have been hugged all these years, and I still want that moment to last forever, the experts tell me I am suffering from separation anxiety and that I should get a dog.

The experts tell me I am too old to experience the joys of love.

After a week of poking, pushing and prodding by several medical specialists it has been confirmed that the Levaquin I've been taking has had no ill side effects,

Old Friends

my Tenormin dosage does not need adjusting and since I can remember every face and friend as far back as the second grade and the only things I have forgotten are the grudges I bore in my youth, I am not even close to being a candidate for Alzheimer's.

My hearing has been tested.

I can still hear raindrops on the window. I can still hear the gentle breathing of the love of my life lying next to me in the night and I can still hear my grandchildren whisper, "I love you" from across the room. I did not take any Ambien but still slept like, well, like a person 50 years younger. My airways are as clear as a mountain stream, my air conditioner works just fine and my serotonin levels are normal.

For the record, I have also had my head examined. I will admit that I was a little anxious about those results, but it turns out I am not suffering from separation anxiety, social anxiety, status anxiety, performance anxiety or any other known anxiety.

And that sedentary lifestyle? Just another way of saying that I have at long last mastered the art of strolling versus strutting and nothing, not even the half moon position, will make me go back to rushing through life.

Shortly after announcing all of this for all the world to hear, the person I have been privileged to share my life with, the love of my life, smiled at me, kissed me gently and gave me that look, that peculiar glance that I thought God had given only to eagles and kings.

My heart raced.
I was at a loss for words.
I got weak in the knees.
I heard the breeze whisper a name.
I was breathless.
I got a silly grin on my face.

I fell madly in love all over again, hoping in my heart that this moment would last forever.

And so to those experts who would say that I am too old to experience the joys of love, I offer up my own opinion.

Love never gets old. Trust me. I'm an expert.

You're as tall as you want to be.
      Marge, who is 83 years old, 58 inches tall and
          can see over mountains.

Uncle Frank

The First Friday

*T*he kid stood staring down at the old man who sat staring up at the kid.
And staring.
And staring.
And staring.
The old man blinked first.

"Anybody ever tell you you've got more freckles than a tiger lily?"
"Freckles are really kisses from angels and if you have a million freckles that means a million angels have kissed you. I know a poem about freckles. Would you like to hear it?"
"No. I'd like you to move so I can see the elephants."
"Today, I stood on my head on my bed and waited and waited and waited but not one single freckle slid out of place. They all stayed put all over my face."
"Very nice, Rembrandt. Now could you move?"
"Rembrandt was a 17th-century Dutch painter. You probably meant to say, 'Very nice, Longfellow.' He wrote Paul Revere's Ride. Would you like to hear it?"
"No. I'd like you to move so I can see the elephants."
"Listen, my children, and you shall hear
Of the midnight ride of Paul Revere,
On the eighteenth of Apr…"
"RAPHI!"

The old man looked up and behind the kid.
The kid spun around.

Old Friends

The woman, pretty in an interesting way, hands on hips, stared first at the kid then at the old man.

"I'm terribly sorry, sir. Is he bothering you?"
"He's a kid. He probably bothers everybody."

Either she didn't know what to say to that or she simply chose to say nothing. Instead, she reached down, took the boy by the hand and walked away.

Quickly.

Without looking back. Although the kid did and called to the old man, "Elephants walk slowly."

The old man watched them disappear into the crowd, shrugged and moved his wheelchair closer to the elephants.

The caregiver came for him 30 minutes later.
Not long after, in his room …
"Would you like to walk, Uncle Frank?"
"Can't walk."
"I'll help you."
The old man felt a hand on his shoulder.
"No!"
He stared straight ahead, steel in his eyes, felt his caregiver grip his shoulder, then loosen his grip, pat him on the shoulder and leave.
Quiet now.
Alone with the thoughts he couldn't push away. Thoughts of another time, another day.

> *"Would you like to walk, Dad?"*
> *"Can't walk."*
> *"I'll help you."*
> *"No!"*

"There's nothing to be afraid of, Dad."
"You'll find out!"

The wind chimes on the patio of the room next door beckoned him back, gently, like the song of an angel.
"Humph!"

The Next Friday
The old man hadn't noticed how small the kid was. Small? How about frail? You'd have to shake the sheets to find him.

"You're back."
"We always come here on Friday."
"Anybody ever tell you you could hang a hat on those ears?"
"I have short hair. It makes my ears appear to be large."
"Elephant ears."
"Anatomically that's not possible. Have you ever studied an elephant's ears?"
"I could if you would move."

The kid took two steps to his right, giving the old man a clear view of three bull elephants, all around five tons each, all conveniently flapping their ears.

"An elephant's ears are full of blood vessels. When they flap their ears, it can lower the temperature of the blood in their ears by as much as 40 degrees."
"What are you? Some sort of whiz kid?"
"Why are you in a wheelchair?"
"My legs quit on me. They're taking the rest of my life off. So, *are* you one of them whiz kids?"
"I'm supposed to be a …"

"RAPHI!"

The same woman who had whisked the boy away last Friday.

"Again, I apologize for him bothering you."
"He wasn't bothering me. He was teaching me about elephant ears."

Either she didn't know what to say to that or she simply chose to say nothing. She did, however, give him a half smile that, on her face, looked pretty good. Then she reached down, took the boy by the hand and walked away, quickly, without looking back, although the kid did. And smiled and waved and called to the old man, "Elephants walk slowly."
The old man nodded to the kid, watched them disappear into the crowd, shrugged and moved his wheelchair closer to the elephants.

The caregiver came for him 30 minutes later.
Not long after, in his room ...
"Do you feel it, Uncle Frank?"
"Feel what?"
"Spring. It's all around us. Let's go for a walk."
"Can't walk."
"You could try. I'll help you."
"No! Leave me alone!"
Alone.
With the thoughts that never left him alone.

> "Do you smell it, Dad?"
> "What?"
> "Spring. Remember? You always told me you could tell it was spring just by breathing it in."

He remembered. Didn't say so.

> "I can smell the earth coming alive again, Dad. That's what you always said, 'I can smell the earth coming alive again.' Come on, let's go walk in it."
> "Can't walk. You know that."

"I don't know that, Dad. Come on, give it a try. What's it going to hurt?"
"You'll find out."

Another Friday.
The kid didn't show. The old man spent his time watching the elephants, trying not to look like he was watching for the kid.
A lot of people were walking around this particular Friday.
"Humph!"
He used to do that. Walk. A lot. Miles every day for most of his life. He lived right, walked right, ate right, did everything right.
And still his body betrayed him.
Heart attack.
How was that possible? Heart attacks weren't supposed to come near people like him. Heart attacks were for everyone else who didn't do everything right. How safe is it to walk into a world as unfair as that?

"You'll find out."

He pulled his father's wheelchair from the garage.
Sat down.
Felt safe.

The Friday After
"Anybody ever tell you that green is not the only color in the world?"
"I know that."
"So how come all you ever wear is green?"
"Green signifies health. Do you like giraffes?"
"Not especially."
"Then how come you're watching them?"
"I'm watching them watch for you so they can warn me when you're coming, give me a chance to get away. You must've sneaked in under their radar."
"Did you know a giraffe heart weighs almost 25 pounds and is two feet long?"
"No, Einstein, I did not know that."

"My name is Raphi. Einstein was a theoretical physicist."
"How do you know all this stuff?"
"My instructor says it's part of my preparation."
"Your instructor? Is that the woman that always shows up out of nowhere to take you away?"
"Yes, but she doesn't show up out of nowhere. She's …"
"RAPHI!"
"… always here."

She didn't look annoyed. More like nervous, uncertain maybe.

"You the instructor?"
"Yes."
"You must be good. The kid knows more than I do."
She smiled. Looked pretty good on her, he thought. "He knows more than anyone."

He didn't know what to say to that. She didn't seem ready to explain. Instead, she reached down, took the kid by the hand and walked away, not quite as quickly as before. More like she was walking and thinking at the same time. That kind of walking slows you down. The kid looked back. Smiled. Waved. And called to the old man, "Giraffes walk slowly."

The old man watched them till they disappeared into the crowd of Friday zoo goers then turned to look up at a giraffe.

"Twenty-five pounds? Really?"

The caregiver came for him 30 minutes later.

Later That Same Friday
"Why have the old man's legs quit on him?"
"They have not quit on him. He quit on them."

The kid tried to digest that. Couldn't.

"He is old, Raphi, and for many like him, with age comes fear. He is no longer the man of his youth and he believes his body has abandoned him. He becomes so convinced that walking is life threatening that his brain actually forgets how to move his legs."
"He quits on his legs?"
"He quits on his life."

Friday Again
"Are you following me?"
"I did not follow you. I preceded you. Did you know the koala is not a bear? It's not even related to a bear. It's related to the kangaroo. They call it a bear because it looks like a teddy bear."
"You are a regular Captain Info today."
"No, I am still Raphi. Did you know that because all they ever eat are eucalyptus leaves, koalas smell like cough drops?"
"Listen, kid, I appreciate all the School at the Zoo stuff you throw at me and I'm getting used to seeing you pop up in front of me in your green shirt every Friday but I just want to sit here in my chair and watch the koalas. Can't you go find someone else to educate?"
"Your legs didn't quit on you. You quit on them."
"What?"
"You're old and you think that's a death sen …"
"RAPHI! STOP!"

Before anyone could say anything more, the instructor grabbed the kid's hand and half ran, half walked away from the koala exhibit and the old man in the wheelchair. The kid turned and shouted, "Koalas move slowly and there's nothing wrong with that."

Only after they had disappeared did the old man realize his feet were planted solidly on the ground. Anyone watching would think he was either getting into his wheelchair or getting out.

The caregiver came for him 30 minutes later. He did not say a word.
Not long after …
"Nice evening for a walk, Uncle Frank."
"Can't walk."
"I can help you."
His caregiver held out a hand.
"No!"
There was music coming from somewhere down the hall.
An old, sad song.
Before he had a chance to lock it out, the old, sad song got inside him and tugged him back to another time.
A sad time.

> "Let's dance, Dad."
> "Can't dance. Can't walk."
> "I think you can, Dad. Try it. There's nothing to be afraid of."
> "You'll find out!"
> "Okay. We'll dance anyway."

He remembered.
Spinning his father's wheelchair around the room in a haphazard rhythm with the old, sad song. Round and round the room they went, one on his toes, one on his haunches in a chair. A wheelchair.
The music stopped.
The dance stopped.
The man kissed his father.

> "I love you, Dad."

Two weeks later, the man's father passed away.
In his wheelchair.

The Last Friday
"Did you know it would take a sloth nearly a month to walk a single mile?"

"Do I know you?"

"Yes. It's been a month and I've changed a little. Most of the freckles are gone and I've put on some weight but look, same green shirt."

"This is a joke, right?"

"No. It's really me. Raphi. Einstein. Rembrandt. Captain Info. Whiz Kid. Elephant Ears. Except look!" He pulled on his ears. "Not so big now that I have more hair." He did have more hair. A lot more, long, almost to his shoulders.

"Look, I saw the kid a month ago. The *kid*. Get it? Nobody goes from a kid to a Jolly Green Giant in a month."

"I would try to explain it to you but it would take too long and you probably still wouldn't believe it so let me just say that I have a message for you. And a gift."

The old man started to say something. The man in green held up his hand.

"Please, just listen." He took a breath. "Life didn't stop. It slowed. The pace changed to accommodate slightly smaller steps. And your body isn't what it used to be. It slows you down. Gets you down. Sometimes even lets you down."

He smiled. Put his hand on the old man's shoulder.

"Elephants move slowly. Giraffes move slowly. Koalas move slowly. The sloth moves slowly. But they all keep moving. You're still in the game, old man. Don't let it frighten you. Let it challenge you. Finish the journey on your terms and …" He handed him a cane. "On your own two feet."

He stepped back, smiling.
"Who *are* you?"
"I am Raphi. Malach."
The old man blinked. Raphi was gone.
Not long after, in his room.
"You feel like walking today, Uncle Frank?"
A pause.

Dance with me, Dad.

He gripped the cane with both hands.
"Uncle Frank?"

Dance with me.

"Sir?"
He lowered the cane to the floor.

Dance ...

Struggled to his feet, the cane wobbling beneath his grip.
"Uncle Frank? Are you wanting to walk?"
"No. I want to dance."
Somewhere, as near as the coming moment yet as far away as forever, the Heavens were rocked with an explosion of joy and an angel named Raphi danced.
Like a child.

❖

"That's my story."
"Quite a story."
"Yeah, and it turns out *malach* is Hebrew for messenger or angel and you're an angel doc, so here I am."
"I'm not an 'angel doc'. I'm an angelologist."
"Whatever. But you know angels, right?"
"I know angels."
"So, who's Raphi?"
"I believe he is the archangel Raphael, the healing angel. His name literally means *God heals* or *He who heals*. And he is usually surrounded by the color green.

"A kid angel? A kid *healing* angel? I thought angels were ten feet tall with wings and harps."

"If you go looking for an angel, don't go looking in the sky. And if you wait to hear a rush of wings you may pass an angel by."

"Which means?"

"Which means angels can manifest themselves in as many ways as you can imagine and many more that you can't."

"Humph! What about the instructor?"

"Probably there to give credibility that you were dealing with a well-trained angel."

"Humph. I don't know."

"Look, an angel brought you a message. Someone cares enough, loves you enough to want to see you believing in yourself again, in life again. Leave it at that."

They talked awhile longer, the old man and the angelologist. In the end, the old man agreed to at least give some thought to the possibility that the impossible had happened. Then he stood, gripped his cane and walked, slowly, to the door.

"Remember."

The old man paused, hand on the doorknob, waiting for the punch line.

"Life slows. It doesn't stop."

Dignity

Is **Rebecca**, helpless in the unrelenting grip of Parkinson's, asking me to help her get a good grip on the spoon in her hand so she can eat her strawberry Jell-O. We both know that most of the Jell-O will end up on her lap, on the table, on the floor, but still she will smile and say, "That's the best strawberry Jell-O I've ever had."

Holy Ground

She'd felt him again. She didn't tell anyone.

Except Pete. She told Pete everything.

"I felt him, Pete. As sure as I felt him next to me all those nights, all those years until..." She stared out at the ocean, not ready to say it yet.

"Did he say anything?"

"No. But I felt him."

She closed her eyes, remembering. Smiled.

"Do you feel the peace?"

She thought about that. Yes, she did feel the peace. It settled over her, cocooned her like a seed in the womb.

Peace.

Not of mankind. Not of womankind. Not of any kind she could remember. A high and holy peace, beyond the barriers of imagination.

"How have I never known peace like this before, Pete? Is it something from God? You know, to help me through all of this?"

Silence. She turned. Pete was gone. He did that — just left without a word.

Her gaze returned to the ocean. Her husband, John, her forever partner, was an ocean man.

"You can't drink it, you can't take a bath in it but by all that God made, this ocean water will cleanse your soul."

She didn't know how long she stood there letting the soul-cleansing ocean heave wave after wave at her feet. Time didn't mean anything anymore. Not since … she couldn't say it yet. Finally, in perfect rhythm with the waves, she heaved a sigh of her own and moved slowly down the beach.

Her husband, John, her forever partner, was a beach man.

"If the ocean cleanses your soul, the beach settles your mind. It's holy ground"

He'd walk his holy ground for miles. She was always waiting at the end of those miles. She closed her eyes. Maybe, like in the movies, she'd open them and see John, strolling toward her. She opened her eyes. She didn't see her husband. She left.

He came to her again.

"Is it normal, Pete?"

They were back on the shore.

"Everything's normal sooner or later."

A hint of quiet wedged itself between them.

"Do you hear them?"

She did hear them, what seemed to her like thousands upon thousands of voices, singing with immeasurable joy, love, honor, exultation and glory. Within a heartbeat, she found herself twirling in circles, like a child in a snowfall trying to catch the flakes on her tongue, letting the voices flow through her like she was made of gauze, feeling, as Dickens put it, "as light as a feather, as happy as an angel, as merry as a school-boy, as giddy as a drunken man."

Above it all, she heard a joyous noise. Coming from her.

Breathless, she asked, "Where are they, Pete? *Who* are they?"

Silence. Pete was gone. He did that – just left without a word.

She didn't know him that well. He'd come into her life not long after … she still couldn't bring herself to say it. Her husband, John, her forever love, had so many friends she had assumed Pete was one of them, there to help her through this most confusing time.

Still catching her breath, she looked down to find herself waist deep in the soul - cleansing ocean. It did not alarm her. It warmed her. She stood, motionless, feeling the ebb and flow, the rhythm. How many times had she stood in the ocean and not felt the rhythm? But it was there, and it was there, in that moment, that the realization came to her.

Rhythm.

She almost believed she could count each grain of sand skipping across her feet in perfect rhythm with the currents tugging them toward the shore then nudging them backward to the sea, in perfect rhythm with the blood weaving its way through her body, in rhythm with the beating of her heart, in rhythm with the air moving in and out of her lungs.

Rhythm.

How had she not noticed this before? She began to sway, gracefully, like a reed sways in the breeze, in perfect rhythm with the ocean zephyr sifting through her hair, in perfect rhythm with the clouds slipping across the sky, in perfect rhythm with the pull of the sun and the moon and the stars.

Rhythm.

Of the rain and the snow and the leaves tumbling from their summer home.

Rhythm.

Everything in existence in perfect rhythm, like an exquisite timepiece, an impossibly orchestrated universe. How had she lived as long as she had and not noticed it? Something new to wonder about as she waded from the ocean onto the beach, singing, well more like whispering, "We are standing on holy ground and there are angels all around." Not exactly the way it was written, but close enough. John would approve.

She closed her eyes, hoping when she opened them she'd see her husband strolling toward her. Just like in the movies. She didn't. She left.

And he came to her again.

Back on the beach with Pete.

"Did I tell you we spent our last New Year's Eve on top of a mountain?" She didn't wait for an answer. " Just before midnight, we wrapped a blanket around us and stood outside and looked up at the stars and promised we'd love each other every day from then on as though it was our last day together. I mean, we always loved each other but it wasn't until ..." she still couldn't say it ... "*this* happened that I realized how much of each other we'd missed over the years. *Life* just got in the way of love. Good Lord, Pete, we wasted so much time."

"Maybe *lost* would be a better word. You lost so much time."

And then there was no more time. No slumbering past. No revolving years. No broad wings of time. No beginning. No middle. No end.

"Pete?"

He was gone. He'd be back.

As many times as she needs me, Pete thought. Some took to it right away. Others took … well … longer. He smiled. Even he forgot now and then. There is no *longer*. No beginning, no middle, no end. Not here.

On the other side of life, where there *is* a beginning, a middle and an end, John ran his fingers over a photo of his forever love. He would have gladly taken on her illness as his own, her pain as his own.

Her death as his own.

Is it possible for love to bind two souls so tightly as to transcend all boundaries, even those between here and hereafter? Could she still feel him? Still feel his forever love? He was sure she could. As sure as the ocean cleansed his soul and the beach, his holy ground, settled his mind.

I still believe I can help people. Sometimes I can't but sometimes I can. I believe that.

May, who, at 89, is not always certain of where she is but knows exactly where she's going.

The Closing Pages

I am an old woman.
    A book.
Nearing its final chapter.

These closing pages are for you.
My daughter.

I may not always have been a good listener.
But I have always heard you
I heard you tapping at my heart before you were born.
I heard every tear you wept for me in the night.
I heard you sing of your dreams while you were awake.
I heard you sigh in your dreams while you slept.
I heard your tears from behind closed doors.
I heard your laughter mingled with the joy of life.
I heard the struggle between the girl you were and the woman you were becoming.
I heard your needs and your wants.
And tried to teach you the difference.
And I never slept until I heard you come home.
Safe.

The times you tried to drive me away, the only thing that kept me there was you.

The times you thought you were my least favorite child were the times I loved you most.

The times you thought you did not please me were the times I was most pleased that you were trying,

There may have been times you thought I was too wrapped up in my own feelings to worry about yours.
But I have always felt you.
I felt your heart beating next to mine.
I felt your impatience as you wanted to be heard before you had words to speak.
I felt your hand in mine, holding tight as you learned to walk.
I felt your fear when I let go.
And your triumph when you learned to stand on your own.

I felt your strength in your weakest moments.
I felt your eyes love me.
Challenge me.
Dare me.
Defy me.
Test me.
Trust me.
Hate me.
Love me again.

The times you thought I didn't love your father were the times I was trying to teach him that he was raising a daughter, not a queen.

The times you said I made you feel miserable, I felt more miserable. And I learned that misery is perhaps the strongest of all bonds.

The times you complained that I wanted you to be someone you weren't, I was showing you that you can be someone you never realized, believed, dreamed you could be.

So many times I felt like a piece of a puzzle in the wrong box but I look at you now and the picture is complete.

And when you are an old woman.
A book.
Nearing its final chapter.
Read these pages once again.
And you will know.

Although I have failed at more things than I have succeeded at, you are not one of them.

I think Southerners would like rugby. It's like dumping a bucket of corn on a field and turning 12 hogs loose.
>Roger, who is 87 and thinks Monday's coffee tastes better on Tuesday.

Birds of A Feather

The birds had gathered.
Four of them, anyway.
Edna, Franny, Louise and George.
The early birds.
Ida, as usual, was late.

> Edna: "Here she comes. Holy cow! Birds, take a deep breath and look up."
> Franny and Louise: "Why?"
> Edna: "Don't look now but Ida has her …"
> Franny and Louise: "Holy cow!"

They took a deep breath and looked up. It was what they did, these birds of a feather, when they found themselves not knowing what to do next. Take a deep breath and look up.

> George: "Why'd she do that?"
> Franny: "We don't know, George, and stop staring!"

George *couldn't* stop staring. *No one* could stop staring.
Edna's face went as red as an Arizona sunset.
Louise's face went as white as a Colorado winter.
Franny's face went as red *and* white as an Italian tablecloth.
George just kept on staring.

An eternity later, a blissfully unaware Ida took her regular seat at her regular table.

> Ida: "Good evening, birds."
> Edna: "Ida, are you feeling alright?"
> Ida: "I'm feeling especially alright because tonight is Lamb Chops Wednesday."

It was Prime Rib Friday but no one said so.

> Franny: "I like your dress. It looks very ... "
> Louise: "Reversible."
> Ida: "Thank you. I dressed in such a hurry, I was afraid it might look like something I threw on at the last minute. Good evening, George."
> George: "Hello, Ida. How are ... things?"

Edna poked Franny, who poked Louise, who poked George, hard, in the ribs and hissed, "Stop staring!"

Other whispers, oily whispers, took wing around the dining room like a secret about a new minister. Edna listened for only a minute before abruptly standing and mumbling, "Birds of a feather." She circled the dining room like an angry wasp and then buzzed out the door. Moments later ...

> Franny: "Holy cow! She didn't!"
> Louise: "Holy cow! She did!"

George could only stare.
"They want to cluck, " Edna announced, retaking her seat, "Let's give them something to cluck about."

> Ida: "Edna, are you alright? You seem a little agitated?"
> Edna: "I love you, Ida, like Sears must have loved Roebuck. Let's leave it at that."

Then a stern look at Louise and Franny and a curt, "Birds of a feather, ladies."

> Louise: "I love you, too, Ida. Will you excuse me a moment, please?"
> Franny: "I'll go with you. Lord knows I can't do this alone."
> George: "Edna, I've never seen you like this."
> Edna: "Put a lid on it, George. And stop staring."

Moments later, after Louise and Franny returned, the four birds of a feather ages 83 (Edna), 87 (Louise), 85 (Franny) and 91 (Ida) ate dinner, told stories they'd told a hundred times before and laughed as hard as the first 99 times. George, every bit of 88, with so much to stare at, had little to say.

After dinner, the four friends linked arms and, for added effect, skipped out of the dining room.

No one talks about the day Ida showed up for dinner wearing her bra over her dress. *Everyone* talks about the day Ida, Edna, Franny and Louise showed up for dinner wearing their bras over their dress. And Edna, Franny, Louise and Ida wouldn't have it any other way.

Ida had been slipping a little more each day. The other birds needed to be there for her, *would* be there for her, and each other. Forever.
Birds of a feather who loved each other like Sears must have loved Roebuck.

They say it took several weeks before George wiped that silly grin off his face.

Courage

Is **Alice,** who asks, "Ask me how I'm feeling today" and, without waiting for an answer, she'll say, "I'm feeling as fine as a frog's hair split 84 ways and you know frogs don't have a lot of hair." Then she will smile that smile that lights up every heart around her, even though the light in her own heart grows dimmer every day.

Spirit

The endurance and strength of rocks, mountains and trees,
Earth is considered the ultimate feminine element.

She sat, no more than 20 feet from the creek, running fast and fat with melted snow, eyes closed, as still as the rocks around her, absorbing the night. The dark did not touch her. The cold did not touch her. The wind touched her, but gently and with reverence, reaching under her hat to sift through her silvery hair, only to be able to say that it had.

"She is earth" would be the tune it would carry through the canyon. "Rare, to be sure."

Rare indeed.

"A rare bird" the doctors all admitted. Easier that than having to admit they had no answer to why she was still alive. She was, after all, 120 years old, give or take a year or so.

Rare indeed.

She came here, to this canyon of red rock, whenever she felt the call, which, lately, was more and more. Three of the last five nights. How she was able to be in her room one moment and "simply gone" the next was another question the doctors and others at the home had no answer for but on the mornings they found her missing, they found her here, in this canyon of red rock.

They would come for her in the morning. They would scold her, wrap her in a blanket and take her back.

But tonight, while the others slept, she sat, eyes closed, as still as the rocks around her.

Feeling the wolf.

"I know you're there."

Barely had her words entered the late spring night than the proverb entered her mind. *What is the women's wisdom? To avoid the wolf and stay at home.*

"Humph! I *am* home."

She opened her eyes. Blue. A shade of blue no one had ever been able to describe. Searched the darkness for a rock big enough to hide a wolf.

There were three.

There was Deer Rock, where ancient peacemakers, blessed with the spirit of the deer, had sat awaiting the awareness that would bring peaceful resolutions to tribal disputes.

The second was Sacred Rock, where centuries of women had gathered to form a circle around the rock and pray for the sick and dying, pray for those who would one day take their place in the circle and pray for visions of what was to come.

The third rock had no name, no known history and no reason to be.

Other than perhaps to hide a wolf.

The old woman smiled and struggled to her feet. It took a minute or two before her legs would hold her weight, 94 pounds and dropping. The pain held a determined grip on her bones lately, but she did not acknowledge it. Still smiling, she shuffled over to the rock with no name and no known history, leaned over the top and looked down.

And saw the wolf.

Gray. Female, maybe seven, maybe eight years old, maybe 70 or 75 pounds. Though she lay on her side, she looked to be as much as six feet from snout to tail and about two and a half feet when she was on her feet.

And bleeding from a large wound in her neck.

Her eyes found the eyes of the old woman.

"Not like this," they seemed to say.

The old woman nodded, lowered herself to the ground and crawled around the rock to where the wolf lay.

Their eyes met again, the she and the she-wolf.

"I want to help you," the old woman whispered. "Will you let me help you?"

The she-wolf tried to lift her head. Couldn't. Closed her eyes. Opened them.

The old woman closed her eyes. Opened them. Crawled backward, away from the wolf, pulled herself to her feet and shuffled to a nearby medicine tree, a ponderosa pine, running with sap. She scooped up a handful, shuffled back to where the Gray lay, knelt next to her and coated the wound with the sap.

The bleeding stopped instantly.

Old Friends

The sap would dry by dawn to form a natural bandage over the wound. Again the old woman crawled backward, away from the wolf, pulled herself to her feet and shuffled to the creek. She filled her hat with the cold spring water, returned to where the wolf lay and placed the hat near her snout.

Then sat with her back against the rock with no name, no known history, touching the wolf every now and then with a worn and withered hand.

Just before dawn, she gave the wolf one last reassuring touch and returned to her spot among the rocks, stopping first to kneel before the medicine tree to offer a prayer.

> *Father of all creatures, mother of all life, let your healing peace overtake and overwhelm her. Drive all fear and darkness from her spirit. Renew her strength. Refresh her life.*

As the last words of her prayer left her mouth she blew softly into the air behind them to speed them on their way.

They came for her at dawn, as she knew they would. They wrapped her in a blanket and scolded her for disappearing again. As she knew they would.

"And what is that all over your hands? Is that blood?"

No one noticed she was not wearing her hat.

She slept most of the day. Dreamless. "I have outlived the Dream Weaver," she told one of the doctors who had asked her if she thought perhaps it might be unusual dreams that caused her to wander off at night.

"And on the nights you wander, do you know where you are going?"

"Home."

Rare indeed.

They fed them well at the home. This particular day was BBQ Ribs Tuesday. If anyone noticed the old woman scraping leftovers from every plate brought back to the kitchen into a large trash bag, they didn't say anything. Probably thought she was just trying to help the cleanup crew.

No one noticed her carrying the bag of leftovers back to her room. No one noticed that one of the carving knives was missing from the kitchen. And no one noticed that the old woman was not in her room as the darkness settled in for the night.

The she-wolf was still there behind the rock with no name and no known history.

Still breathing.

She had managed to drink most of the water from the old woman's hat and somehow found the strength to reposition herself so that she now lay with her back pressed into the rock. She watched in silence as the old woman approached, got down on her hands and knees, opened the bag and placed the leftover rib bones in a pile in front of the she-wolf's snout. She retrieved her hat and, still on hands and knees, never taking her eyes from the she-wolf's eyes, backed away. Once she was on the other side of the rock with no name and no known history, the old woman struggled to her feet and shuffled, hat in hand, to the creek where she filled the hat with fresh cold spring water. She moved then to the medicine tree, the ponderosa pine and, taking the carving knife from her pocket, cut very carefully into the bark.

Pine trees are made up of layers. The layer the old woman was digging for was the thin dark cambium layer rich with vitamins and nutrients. She cut a few small pieces the she-wolf would instinctively chew, then a few more that she would take back to the home and boil into a more easily digestible mush.

Satisfied that she had enough, she scooped up a handful of sap and smoothed it over the wound she had made in the tree then shuffled back to where the she-wolf lay, got down on her hands and knees and placed the water near her snout. The animal did not move but never took her eyes from the old woman.

The rib bones lay untouched where she had left them. She picked one up. Leaned back against the rock with no name, no known history and looked straight ahead.

"I had a dog once that loved to chew on bones, but what he loved even more was when I held the bone for him while he chewed." As she spoke, she positioned the bone near the she-wolf's mouth.

"I'm not going to say he was lazy, I'm just going to say I think he …"

She felt a tug on the bone. Held it tight. Felt the bone being crushed by the same teeth that could crush every bone in her hand. Let it go. Reached for another, held it out, felt it being tugged and crushed.

"… appreciated a little help now and then."

Within minutes, every bone had been crushed and swallowed. The old woman smiled.
Then came the sound of water being lapped from the old woman's hat, slowly, probably painfully.

Then the quiet.

The old woman handed the pine bark to the she-wolf. She took it, held it in her mouth, and chewed slowly.

More quiet.

"My name is D. Just a single letter. It is what my husband called me. Don't know your name but I believe I'll call you Spirit."

"My husband is gone now. He knew me better than anyone and he hardly knew me at all. I think he respected me more than understood me."

D looked at Spirit. Spirit looked back.

"To my mind, it's good to be a woman brave and strong with a little bit of adventure thrown in. He accepted me for being all of that but he also knew I would be there whenever he needed me. And I knew he would be there whenever I needed him. He let me be independent and with him at the same time. He wasn't a real affectionate man but every now and then he would kiss me and tell me he admired my courage and strength and sense of adventure. When he passed, his last words to me were 'I allowed the world to control me. Don't let it control you, D.'"

Far away, a wolf howled.

Spirit's eyes flickered then seemed to fill with sadness. It was not her mate calling. Her mate lay dead on a hill by a hunter's bullet, the same hunter whose bullet was still lodged in the she-wolf's neck. No more would be the days when her mate would nuzzle her for seemingly no reason other than perhaps to tell her he admired her bravery and strength and sense of adventure whenever they hunted together. He knew she would be there for him in times of danger, and she was, trying to drag him out of more harm's way when the second bullet found its way into her neck. And he was there for her, rising up and throwing himself on top of her as the third bullet found its way to his heart. She did not want to leave him. Theirs was a life-long bond and until that moment they were inseparable. But the last thing she saw before the light left his eyes was his final message to her: *Run. Do not let them have both of us.*

They sat quietly the rest of the night, the she and the she-wolf. Just before dawn, D gave Spirit one last reassuring touch and returned to her spot among the rocks, stopping first to kneel before the medicine tree to offer a prayer.

Father of all creatures, mother of all life, let your healing peace overtake and overwhelm her. Drive all fear and darkness from her spirit. Renew her strength. Refresh her life.

As the last words of her prayer left her mouth she blew softly into the air behind them to speed them on their way.

They came for her at dawn, as she knew they would. They wrapped her in a blanket and scolded her for disappearing again. As she knew they would.

"Do you know you could be eaten alive by wolves out here?"

She knew there was a better chance that she could sprout wings and fly than to be eaten alive by a wolf.

No one noticed she was not wearing her hat.

She slept into the afternoon. Dreamed of how old she was. Not in years but in heart, mind and soul. Saw herself on a path. Looked behind her, saw she had been alone on that path most of her life. Looked ahead. Saw Spirit. Waiting.

"Guess I haven't outlived the Dream Weaver after all," she muttered to herself upon waking.

She spent a good amount of what was left of the afternoon boiling the tree bark into a mush. That evening, she collected a bag of leftover pork chops.

By dark, she was back in the canyon, leaning against the rock with no name and no known history watching Spirit eat leftover pork chops dipped in cambium mush. Afterward, the she-wolf found the strength to sit and drink the cold spring water D had collected in her hat. Then she lay next to where the old woman sat and closed her eyes.

"I had kids. Three of 'em."

Spirit opened her eyes, looked at the old woman gazing off into another time and place.

"Raised them to always be curious, always ask questions, always keep learning. Brought them here to this part of the world where they could learn to respect the earth and everything in it and on it and above it. Always wanted a good place to raise them. Taught them that family was more important than anything. We never had a lot but we always had each other. Always loved each other. Any one of us would have died for any one of them. My husband used to say he wished he could build a bubble and put all of us in it forever."

D fell silent. Let a tear slip. Spirit cocked her head.

"It was hard letting them go." She looked at the wolf. "You're a mother. You know."

She did know. It fell on her to lead the pack to where it was safest to raise her pups. Wolf pups are born blind and deaf, completely reliant on their parents and the pack to raise them. She would protect them with her life if necessary. She would spend 10 months teaching them to always be curious but cautious, always be aware of where they were, always respect the earth and everything in it, on it and above it. After the first few weeks, every wolf in the pack joined in to help raise and nurture the pups. Before they were even a year old, the mother reluctantly pushed them from the den to begin hunting with the rest of the family.

They sat quietly the rest of the night, the she and the she-wolf. Just before dawn, D gave Spirit one last reassuring touch and returned to her spot among the rocks, stopping first to kneel before the medicine tree to offer a prayer.

> *Father of all creatures, mother of all life, let your healing peace overtake and overwhelm her. Drive all fear and darkness from her spirit. Renew her strength. Refresh her life.*

As the last words of her prayer left her mouth she blew softly into the air behind them to speed them on their way.

They came for her at dawn, as she knew they would. They wrapped her in a blanket and scolded her for disappearing again. As she knew they would.

"When is this going to end?"

No one noticed she was not wearing her hat.

Spirit was in her dreams again. On the same path as D, but farther away than in the last dream, beckoning to the old woman as if to say, "Hurry. This way home." She did not question the dream, nor did she question the bond drawing the two of them deeper and deeper into each other. They were both, after all, female, both intuitive, both survivors.

Both earth.

Hours later, when all in the home were asleep in their beds, D was once again in the canyon sitting with her back against the rock with no name, no known history watching Spirit eat the leftover meatloaf she'd brought.

"Do you ever feel old, Spirit? I do. Old and tired. I think it's because of all the thinking I do. All the observing and wondering and figuring and life learning and all the trying to pass it along to anyone who might get it, get *me*. In the end, it's all about love and peace. Pretty simple. Most people don't get it. It's too easy I guess."

She was quiet awhile. Thinking again.

"I have had a life." She spoke softly, her hand resting on Spirit's neck, feeling the she-wolf's energy beginning to slip away. "I have had a man stand by me, steadfast even through the times we tried to drive each other away. I have taken his strength when I needed it, given him mine when he needed it. Shared joy and pain and hunger and gain and grief and a different belief. Shared heart and soul. I have felt children sleep to the beat of my heart and I to theirs. I have felt their joy and their pain, held them through bumps and bruises and broken bones and broken hearts and sweetness and sorrow and everything they could come up with." She paused. Smiled. "Or down with. I always told them, feel good or feel bad. Your choice."

She paused again.
"I have caught rain and snow on my tongue and tasted life. I have stood on the top of mountains and I have sunk deep into the mud. I have sat on a cloud and closed my eyes and let the wind give me wings. In my dreams I have seen the world through God's eyes.

I have had a life that taught me to accept one truth. What is, is."

Spirit shifted and lay her head on D's lap. Felt the old woman's energy beginning to slip away. Felt herself slipping away, beyond this rock with no name, no known history, beyond the hill where her mate lay victim to hunter's bullets, beyond now.

To then.

Then, with the wind in her face as the two of them, forever mated, ran wild just to feel the joy of running wild. Then, when they hunted as a team and together took down prey two and three times their size. Then, when they shared good times and withstood hard times, together, always together, never turning their back to each other's needs and wants.

There were pups. Three litters. All of them raised with fierce love and dedication to a single knowing. What is, is. No wolf, no animal, no bird, no living creature has ever tried to change what is. They simply deal with it and, almost like it was planned, achieve a perfect balance. They live in the moment, love in the moment, treasure the moment, *are* the moment.

There were times when she and her mate stood and howled for no other reason than to express their acceptance of what is, is.

They sat quietly, leaning against each other the rest of the night, the she and the she-wolf. Just before dawn, the old woman gave the wolf one last reassuring touch and returned to her spot among the rocks, stopping first to kneel before the medicine tree to offer a prayer.

> *Father of all creatures, mother of all life, let your healing peace overtake and overwhelm us both. Drive all fear and darkness from within each of us. Let tomorrow become today.*

As the last words of her prayer left her mouth she blew softly into the air behind them to speed them on their way.

They came for her at dawn, as she knew they would. They wrapped her in a blanket and scolded her for disappearing again. As she knew they would.

"D, this has to end now!"

No one noticed she was not wearing her hat.

Spirit was in her dreams again. On the same path as D, but this time at her side. In the distance ahead, she thought she saw a man standing next to a wolf. Waiting. D saw herself put her hand on Spirit's head and the two of them stepped forward.

Toward home.

She did not take food with her that night. She did not take water, she did not take sap or bark from the medicine tree. Instead, she lay closer than ever to Spirit, curled up in her middle. They lay there together, against the rock with no name, no known history.

The she and the she-wolf.

Separable and inseparable.

Like night and day.

Heaven and earth.

Life and death.

The old woman began to feel the peace run through her; the peace that lies just beyond the door into eternity.

Within seconds, the she-wolf felt the same peace.

Their hearts stopped beating at exactly the same moment.

When they came for her at sunrise, D was not there. After weeks of searching, all they found was her hat. Most agreed that a wolf probably carried her off.

Years passed.

A young boy, visiting the canyon of red rock, pointed to a rock. A rock with no name and no known history.
"Look, Mama, do you see the shape of the lady and the wolf in the rock?"

Life's like furniture. You have to move it around a little now and then. Get a fresh look.
>Reva, who is 86 and wears a different dress to dinner every evening.

The Letter

*I*f you could read between the lines on her face, you would know more than anyone in the home.
None of them knew how old she was.
Not for sure, anyway.
Some guessed a hundred years.
Some guessed more.
A lot of people in the home had an opinion on that.
But because she never spoke, no one could be positive.
And since no one ever came to visit, there was no one to ask.

The one thing that most people in the home agreed upon was that she had no memory of anyone, anything, any life.
But because she never spoke, no one could be positive.
And since no one ever came to visit, there was no one to ask.

She spent most days sitting by the window, a Bible balanced upon her knee. A Bible as old and as worn as she. At least three times a day, she opened the Bible, took out the letter, read it, smiled and then carefully placed it back between the sacred pages. This was the second time today. She read:

> *You were called upon.*
> *Again and again.*
> *You were asked for love at times when you yourself were asking for love.*
> *And you gave it.*

Old Friends

You were needed, even when you yourself needed.
And you were there.
You were asked for answers when you yourself were filled with questions.
And you answered.

You were expected to be always strong and even as you wondered where the strength would come from, you found it.
You were asked to make things better. You didn't know how.
But you did it.
You were asked to hold even when you, yourself needed to be held.
And you did it.

There were times you were frightened.
You were alone.
You had doubt and you wanted out.
But only you ever knew.
You were there from the beginning.

She paused.
Remembered the needs.
The questions.
The weak moments.
The fears.
The sleepless nights.
The doubts.
Remembered how empty she felt at times.
How lonely.
Like a deserted house.
Was it worth it?
Did any of it matter?

She read the rest of the letter.

You are my mother. There is no one else like you in the world.
Thank you.
I love you.

She smiled.
Then carefully placed the letter back between the sacred pages.
Next to the Medal of Honor.
No one knew anything about the letter.
A lot of the people in the home had an opinion.
But because none of them could read between the lines on her face and because the lady, who spent most days sitting by the window with a Bible balanced upon her knee, a Bible as old and as worn as she, never spoke, no one could be positive.

And because no one ever came to visit, there was no one to ask.

I believe in magic. I don't see any right now but I know it's there. That's what makes it magic.
      Anne, who is 91 and still does card tricks.

I'll Fight the World

"I'll fight the world for you, Ellie, I'll fight the world."
He was 12.
She was 10.
Or was he 11, she 9?
Hard to remember those days, these days.

"You can't fight the world, Danny. It's too big."

Danny and Ellie.
As much in love as a 12-year-old and a 10-year-old could be in love.
Or was that 11 and 9?
Either way, they promised to love each other forever.

He was 17.
She was 15.
Her father had taken a job all the way east.
Danny stood in the street.
Watching the car disappear.
Ellie disappear.

"I'll fight the world for you, Ellie, I'll fight the world," he called after the car.
"You can't fight the world, Danny," she called back, her head out the window.
"It's too big."
Not long after, Danny's father took a job all the way west.

He was 40.
Living south.
In a life that did not include her.
She was 38.
Living north.
In a life that did not include him.
Yet here they stood, face-to-face.
With a lifetime between them.
Accidental meeting?
Impossible meeting?
Who knows how these things work?
But there they stood.
Face-to-face.

"I was hoping if I ever saw you again, it would mean nothing, that all it ever was, was kid love."
"I was hoping the same thing."
They were both wrong.

They drove.
Parked.
Talked.
And talked.
And talked until dark.
They were in love.
Had been since he was twelve and she was ten.
Or was that eleven and nine?
Either way, they promised to love each other forever.

When there was nothing left to say, Danny flipped the headlights on.
Pushed a tape into the player.
Stepped from the car.
Asked Ellie to dance.

She took his hand.
He took her in his arms, held her close and whispered in her ear.
"I'll fight the world for you, Ellie, I'll fight the world."
She whispered back.
"You can't fight the world, Danny. It's too big."

"Let's watch the sunrise."
They climbed on top of the car and held each other.
She was cold.
He gave her his shirt.
High above, silent witness to a love most can only dream of, the moon hung its head.
And cried.

A heartbeat later the sun rose.
He held her face in his hands.
A touch so gentle it wouldn't put a ripple in a brook.
They kissed.
Goodbye.

She went north.
To a life that did not include him.
He went south.
To a life that did not include her.
Either way, they promised to love each other forever.

He was 82.
She was 80.

Somewhere in the south, in a quiet room, Danny was saying, "I'll fight the world for you, Ellie, I'll fight the world."
One of the women in the room told the other, "It doesn't mean anything. Sometimes he rambles."

Old Friends

Somewhere in the north.

In a quiet room.

She very carefully removes the tissue wrapping from a shirt brought home with her from a visit long ago.

Holds it to her heart.

And with the door locked behind her, where no one could find her, Ellie starts slowly to dance.

Grace

*J*s **Joan**, who doesn't remember much of anything anymore, and the day she told me, "I can't remember how to eat soup, so I'll just eat ice cream."

Love Waits

"Who do you suppose is waiting for us in heaven?"
Janelle always asked the tough questions.

Tough enough to turn the room suddenly quiet.
As though it was empty.
Unusual for this group.
Georgia, Ted, Roger, Helen and William looked at Janelle.
And wondered.
Something they'd probably wondered a hundred times.
But not out loud.
Who *was* waiting?

No gal made has got a shade on sweet Georgia Brown.

It was Georgia.
Singing.
Shaky.
Soft.
Hoarse.

Two left feet but oh so neat has sweet Georgia Brown.

"He would hold me in his big arms, sing that song to me and dance me around like I was the belle of the ball, the love of his life.
And then he died.

I've always felt that he was still here, that he got some sort of pass to leave heaven and come watch over me, watch me live my life.
I hope he's waiting.
I hope the first thing he says to me is, 'You did good, Georgia.'"

She closed her eyes.
Saw her father.
Waiting.
To dance again.
With the belle of the ball.
The love of his life.
And his afterlife.
His sweet Georgia.
Tears rolled across her paper-thin cheeks.

Heaven is full of parents.
Parents lead the way.
In life.
After life.
They go ahead of us.
Give us a light to follow.
Love is the light.
Love is waiting.

"Debbie's waiting."
Anyone who knew Ted knew two things about him.
His nickname was Batman.
His wife's name wasn't Debbie.

"I think about her all the time. Wonder if she's thinking about me. Never got to know her well. Wanted to. Still want to. Always will."

Questions hung in the air.
Ted left them hanging.

He and Debbie were a song.
Unfinished.
Soul mates.
One breathed in.
The other out.
One lost.
One found.
One left.
One stayed.
Both waited.

He closed his eyes.
Saw her there.
Saw him there.
Two people pulled together
Then pulled apart.
Wondered what might have been
If things had been different.
Felt something stir inside him.
Again.
Heaven is full of unfinished love.
Sparks that flew.
But never landed.
Now hovering.
In heaven.
Waiting.
To fly again.

Love, unfinished, is waiting.

"Corned beef and cabbage. That's what we were."

Roger stopped to clear his throat.

"As close as two ticks of the clock. Best friends. We ran away together when we were just kids. Made it as far as Louisville. Then we got hungry and hitched home. But we were gone a week and that got our names in the paper."

He remembered.
Chuckled.

"I moved. He moved. But we stayed in touch, kinda following each other's life through phone calls and letters. When the Internet was invented, we took up emailing. I was corned beef at something or other dot COM. He was cabbage."

He remembered.
Smiled.
Remembered more.
Sighed.
Deeply.

"He got Parkinson's. I called him every week. One week I called and he didn't answer."

He closed his eyes.
Remembered the day he would never forget.
Thought of the day he hoped would come.
"I hope he's waiting."

Heaven is full of friends.
Those who found friendship a richer joy, perhaps, than love.
Always there.
Even when they leave.
Always waiting.
Even now.

Forever friends
Waiting.
Forever.

Helen's face lit up and everyone in the room knew what she was going to say next.

"Henry is waiting."

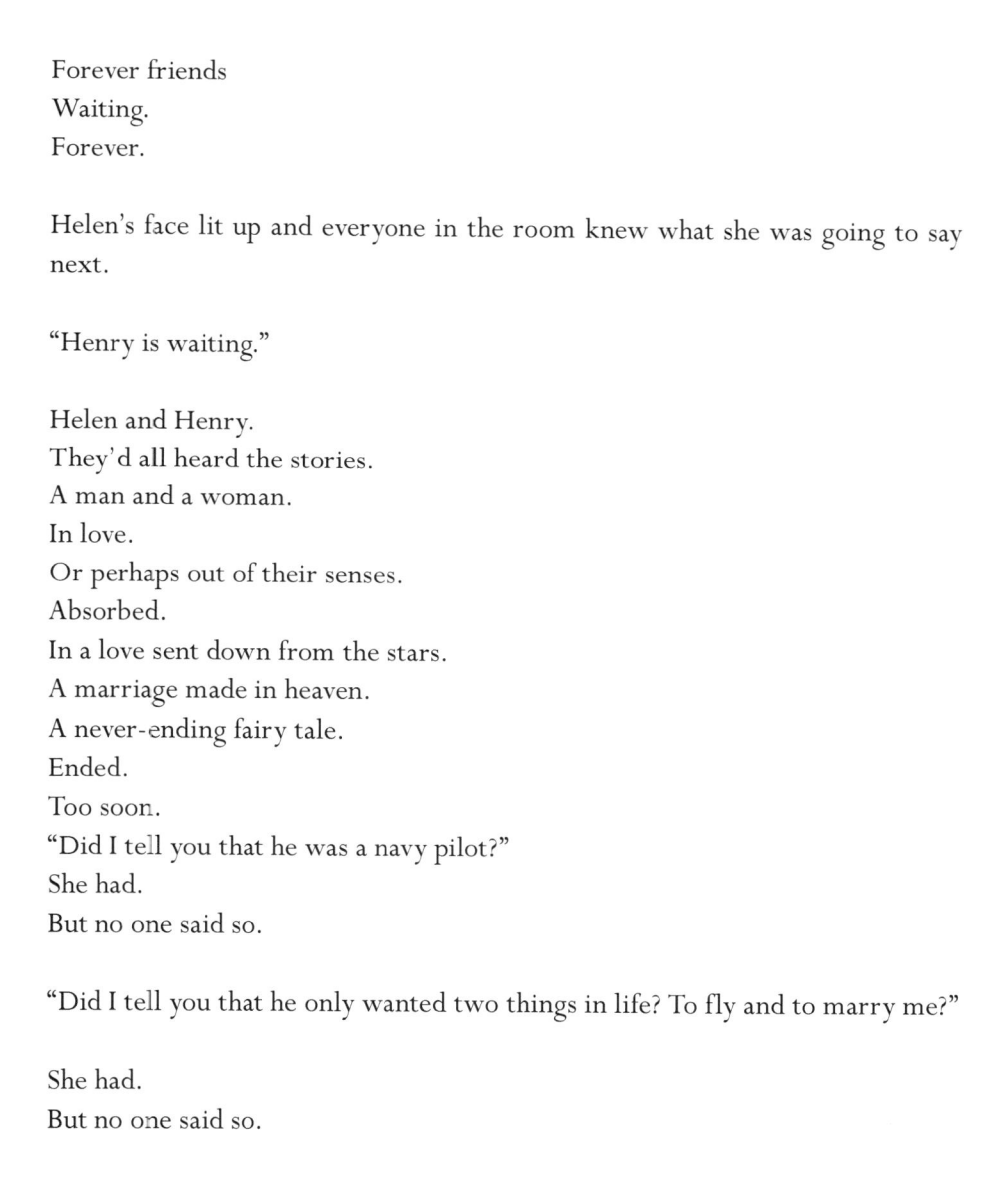

Helen and Henry.
They'd all heard the stories.
A man and a woman.
In love.
Or perhaps out of their senses.
Absorbed.
In a love sent down from the stars.
A marriage made in heaven.
A never-ending fairy tale.
Ended.
Too soon.
"Did I tell you that he was a navy pilot?"
She had.
But no one said so.

"Did I tell you that he only wanted two things in life? To fly and to marry me?"

She had.
But no one said so.

"When I would tell him that flying was too dangerous, he would laugh and say 'Walking through the mud carrying a rifle is dangerous.' And then he'd take my hand and say 'Come fly with me, Helen'.

I'd tell him don't be so silly. How can I fly with you? And he'd say, 'Just because we weren't born with wings doesn't mean that we can't fly.' Then he'd pick me up, twirl me around, and … "

She stopped, lost in the memory of things too private to share.
Closed her eyes.
Thought out loud.

"He didn't say much. He had those looks that said what words never could. But just before he died, he did say something I'll never forget.
Three little words.
'I'll be waiting.'
So, yes. Henry is waiting. And I can't wait to fly with him again."

Heaven is full of husbands.
And wives.
Bound together.
With a love that holds fast.
Holds dear.
Holds hands.
Holds on.
Lets go.
Waits.
To be continued.

William wondered if it was, after all these years, time to say it out loud.
Yes.
Come what may.
"Rocky is waiting for me. Well, maybe not. I just hope that they let me into heaven long enough to find him and tell him how sorry I am that I killed him."

Helen's mouth fell open.
Georgia made that funny noise she makes in her throat.
Ted and Roger looked at each other.

Janelle looked at William, her eyes filled with questions.
Janelle always asked the tough questions.
Sometimes without saying a word.
"I was young, just married, out to conquer the world. Suddenly, Pat, my wife, was pregnant. I wasn't ready for that. It wasn't part of the plan. Not right then, anyway. I tried to block it out, pretend it wasn't happening. Told my wife I didn't want any part of it. But I couldn't change it.

The baby was born. A boy. My son. I didn't even look at him. He was sick. Pat said she'd call him Rocky because he fought so hard. But he didn't make it. My fault. I think he knew I didn't want him. After he died, that's when I started wanting him."

William closed his eyes.
Saw his son.
Wanted him.
Too late.
Heaven is full of children.
Lifted from their parents' arms
Into the arms of an angel.
Forever safe.
In a place where moonbeams tap at their windows
Inviting them out to play
Where they can go riding on cloud-covered ponies
All over the Milky Way.
Heaven is full of children
Forever forgiving.
Forever at play.

Forever young.
Forever alive.
Waiting.
For Mom.
And Dad.

"What about you, Janelle? Who's waiting for you?"
Janelle took the time to look at each of her friends.
Friends who had just shared their most intimate hopes.
Friends she hoped would stay together.
Forever.
With each other.
And with those who waited.
Closed her eyes.
And remembered.

The boy who'd pull her hair.
But beat up any other boy who'd dare.
The boy she waded barefoot with, catching crawdads under the bridge.
Then walked home with.
Hand in hand.
Singing,

> *Yonder comes a man with a sack on his back*
> *Got all the crawdads he can pack.*

The boy all the other girls wanted.
And all the other boys wanted to be.

The boy she fought with, laughed with, cried with.
Wished she'd died with.

"My brother," she said, her eyes still closed.
"My great big war hero brother is waiting."

Old Friends

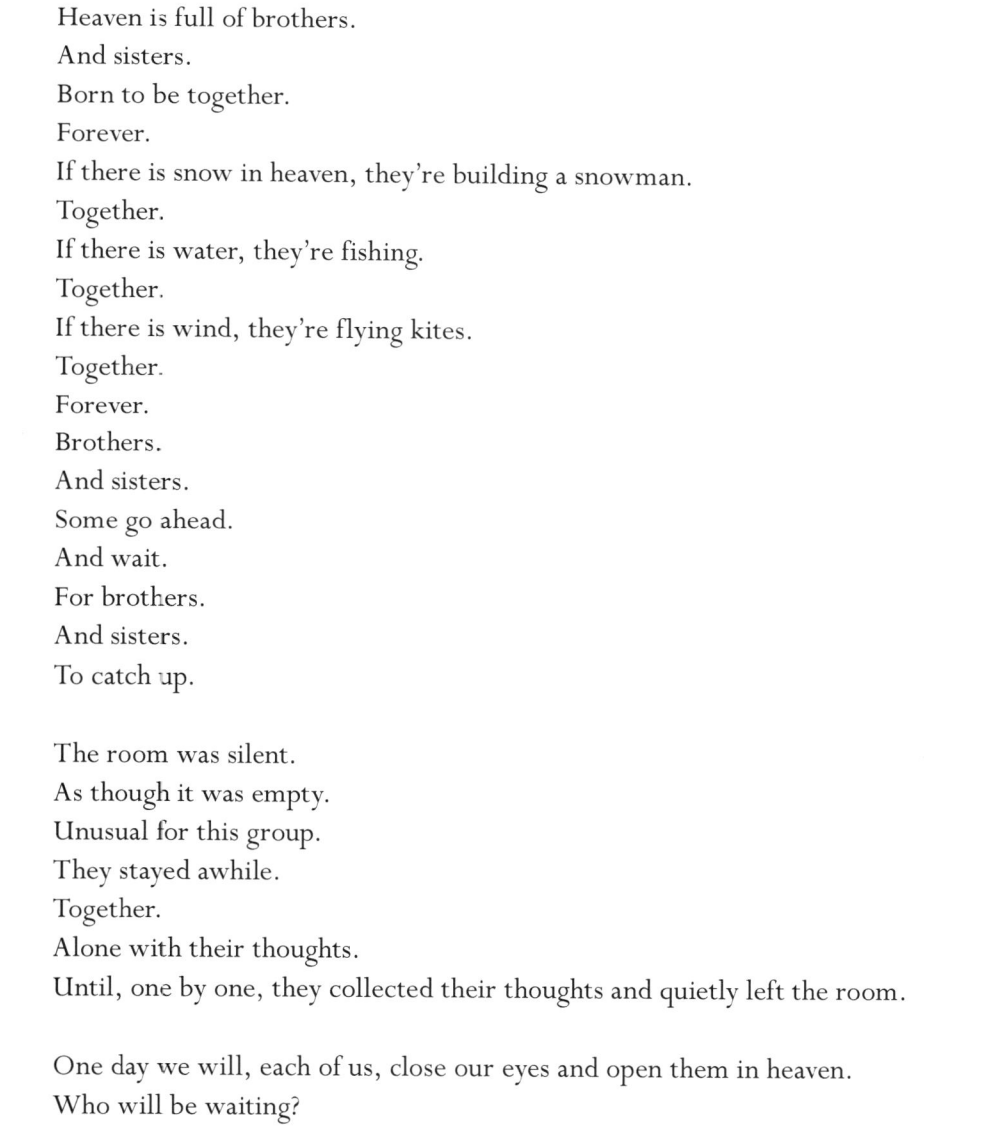

Heaven is full of brothers.
And sisters.
Born to be together.
Forever.
If there is snow in heaven, they're building a snowman.
Together.
If there is water, they're fishing.
Together.
If there is wind, they're flying kites.
Together.
Forever.
Brothers.
And sisters.
Some go ahead.
And wait.
For brothers.
And sisters.
To catch up.

The room was silent.
As though it was empty.
Unusual for this group.
They stayed awhile.
Together.
Alone with their thoughts.
Until, one by one, they collected their thoughts and quietly left the room.

One day we will, each of us, close our eyes and open them in heaven.
Who will be waiting?
What will be waiting?

Perhaps, if we were allowed a glimpse into heaven, we would see that the ties that bind us together were cut from a cloth woven before time began.
A never-ending tapestry of life.

After life.
A tapestry woven with no pain, no sorrow, no tears, no regrets.
Green pastures.
Quiet waters.
Souls restored.
Souls reunited.
Hearts set at rest.
All that and more.
More than we can imagine.
Waiting.
In the sweet by and by.
Each of us will find out.
By and by.

I still believe I'm going to heaven. Not today I hope, but one day. I had an aunt that lived to be 101. Maybe then.

> Colleen, who is 83 and says she has a good 18 years left in her.

Honor

*I*s **Pearl**, who wears one of her husband's bow ties to dinner every evening. Her husband, who passed away several years ago.

I still believe that one day the Wildcats will beat the Crimson Tide.
>Dorman, who is 88 and refuses to die before Kentucky beats Alabama.

And I believe you're crazy.
>Arnie, who is 89 and would rather die than see Kentucky beat Alabama.

William McDonald is an Emmy Award winning writer who, for more than 30 years, specialized in emotional communication in the broadcast industry. For several more years, he was a caregiver in assisted-living homes, memory-care homes and private homes, and it was there that he met many of the old friends who inspired these stories. He writes and blogs at www.oldfriendsendlesslove.com full time from his home in Colorado.